T0193541

Copyright © 2013 Stephen Harley.

All rights reserved. No part of this book may be used or reproduced by any means, graphic, electronic, or mechanical, including photocopying, recording, taping or by any information storage retrieval system without the written permission of the author except in the case of brief quotations embodied in critical articles and reviews.

Inspiring Voices books may be ordered through booksellers or by contacting:

Inspiring Voices
1663 Liberty Drive
Bloomington, IN 47403
www.inspiringvoices.com
844-686-9605

Because of the dynamic nature of the Internet, any web addresses or links contained in this book may have changed since publication and may no longer be valid. The views expressed in this work are solely those of the author and do not necessarily reflect the views of the publisher, and the publisher hereby disclaims any responsibility for them.

Any people depicted in stock imagery provided by Getty Images are models, and such images are being used for illustrative purposes only.
Certain stock imagery © Getty Images.

ISBN: 978-1-4624-0774-3 (sc)
ISBN: 978-1-4624-0775-0 (e)

Print information available on the last page.

Inspiring Voices rev. date: 09/07/2023

InspiringVoices®

To my wife Susie and our lovely dogs Cody and Prince.

THE CHRISTMAS TIME DOG RESCUE

This is the story of a young ten-year old boy named Peter, who lived in Terryville with his parents Gary and Shari Miller. He also lived with his dog Cody. Peter and Cody were very fond of each other.

It was the night before Christmas Eve, and the city was covered with snow. Mr. Miller was out of town with Cody. Mrs. Miller was at home reading the Christmas story to Peter. She read, "On Christmas day, Jesus Christ, God's only Son, was born to Mary and Joseph. He was born in a stable in Bethlehem. He later died for our sins and rose from the dead. When we invite Jesus into our hearts, we become His children."

"Mother," said Peter. "Will Daddy ever receive Jesus like we did and become a Christian?"

Mrs. Miller said, "We must pray that he will."

Soon Mr. Miller walked in the door. "Y'all, I have bad news. Cody ran away from me in Biller City, and I never found him."

Peter began to cry. "Will we ever get him back?"

"I hope so. I called the pound, and they will watch for him. But finding him could be hard. Biller City is a big town with over 200,000 people."

"Well, with prayer we can get him back," said Mrs. Miller.

"Peter," said Mrs. Miller. "We will pray for Cody to be found. You must pray, too. Now go to bed and get some sleep while Daddy and I go shopping. All four of your grandparents are coming over for Christmas tomorrow."

After Peter's parents left, he walked in the garage and found Cody's collar and license tag in the pick-up truck. Peter took them and went inside. Soon the phone rang. Peter answered the phone and found it was his friend Rob Lanes who used to live in Terryville. "Peter!" said Rob. "Does your family not want Cody anymore?"

"We do want him back," replied Peter. "My dad lost him in Biller City."

"Lost him?" laughed Rob. "Your dad went off and left him near the freight yard where I work! He drives a green pick-up truck, doesn't he?"

"Yes," answered Peter.

"Well, I saw your dad let Cody out of the truck and leave him here," said Rob. "I quickly went to get him. He's here in the office."

"Well, I found Cody's collar and tag in the truck!" exclaimed Peter. "How mean of Daddy! He doesn't like dogs!"

"Well, I'm leaving town for Christmas," said Rob. "But the freight yard will keep Cody for you."

"Thanks. Tell them I'll be there some time tomorrow. I'm mad at Daddy for lying to me!" said Peter.

Yes, Peter was very angry with his father for leaving Cody in Biller City and for lying. He packed his knapsack with a box of cereal, dog food, three bottles of water, a blanket, the collar and license, a leash, two dog dishes, and all the money he had saved.

That night, after Peter was sure his parents were asleep, he put on his clothes, jacket and cap. He also put his knapsack on his back. Then he sneaked out the bedroom window leaving a note for his parents.

Peter dashed to a nearby truck garage where a truck driver named Al Parker was getting ready to leave town. "Hello Al," said Peter.

"Peter, why are you out so late?" said the truck driver.

Peter said, "I need to get to the Biller City Freight Yard. My dad dumped my dog there and left him. If you're going that way, I'd like to ride with you."

But Al replied, "Are you sure your dad did that?"

"Yes sir," said Peter. "Rob Lanes called me and told me that he saw the whole thing."

"Oh yes, I know Rob!" exclaimed the truck driver. "But how will you get home? I'll be driving way past Biller City."

"Al, please? I want my dog back!" exclaimed Peter.

"All right," said Al. "Hop in. You can sleep in the sleeper berth behind me. I'll wake you when we get to the freight yard."

As soon as Peter got into the truck, Al drove away. Peter prayed to himself, "Lord Jesus: Please keep Cody safe. Please keep him at the freight yard till I get there. I forgive my father. Please help him become a Christian. Please help Mother and Daddy to let me keep Cody. Thank you for hearing me. Amen."

Biller City was 250 miles away from home. But the ride seemed like no time at all to Peter. He slept until the truck arrived at the freight yard on the morning of Christmas Eve. Al then awoke him. Peter thanked him and got out of the truck. He then dashed into the freight yard office. He quickly saw Cody in there.

"Thanks for keeping him for me!" said Peter happily.

"You are most welcome!" replied the foreman. "Merry Christmas to you!"

"Merry Christmas to you, too!" exclaimed Peter. He put the collar, license tag, and leash on his dog.

Peter took Cody to the bus station to see if he could get a ride home. He said to the desk worker, "Please, Sir. We have no way to get home to Terryville. I do not have enough money to buy a ticket. But I will pay you all the money I have with me if you'll let us on the bus."

The desk worker said, "I would gladly let you on the bus, but no dogs are allowed!"

"But I came from Terryville to get him when he was left here! We have no place to stay!" begged Peter.

"Well I'm sorry, but that's the rule," replied the desk worker.

Peter sadly left the bus station. He walked Cody a few blocks and came to a city bus stop. He fed his dog some food and water. Then he ate some cereal and drank some water. Soon a city bus arrived. Peter asked the driver, "Does this bus go to the truck stop?"

"Yes," answered the bus driver. "But you can't take your dog on the bus."

The bus driver drove off. Peter said, "Cody, if you don't go home, I don't go home! If I call home, Daddy will make me leave you here." He then began to pray, "Lord Jesus: Thanks for helping me to find Cody. Please help us to get home tonight safely. I pray that Mother and Daddy will not be mad at me. Please help them to let me keep Cody. Please help my dad to become a Christian. Amen."

Meanwhile, Mr. and Mrs. Miller found Peter's note. It said, "Daddy, You lied to me about Cody! Leaving him was mean! I'm on my way to Biller City. I'm not coming home without my dog. Your Son, Peter."

Mrs. Miller snapped, "Did you dump Cody out and leave him in Biller City?"

Mr. Miller started crying and said, "Yes I did."

"Gary Miller!" said Mrs. Miller. "You big liar! You are cruel and mean!"

Mr. Miller cried and said, "Yes Shari. I've been so mean to Peter and Cody."

"God does not like it when we mistreat His pets!" said Peter's mother angrily. "Just where did you dump Cody out?"

Peter's father sadly replied, "Near the Biller City Freight Yard. I thought one of the workers would find him and keep him."

"Well, I'll call the freight yard to see if anyone has seen Peter and Cody," said Mrs. Miller. Then she left the room.

Mr. Miller then saw that praying to Jesus was his only hope for his son to make it home. He prayed, "Lord Jesus. I repent I am a sinner. I am sorry for all my sins. I'm sorry I abandoned Cody and for lying to the family. Please come into my heart and guide every part of my life from now on. Also, please bring Peter and Cody home safely today. Thank you Jesus for hearing me. Amen."

Mrs. Miller entered the room and said, "The freight yard foreman said Peter and Cody left hours ago. So I called the police."

Mr. Miller said, "Well Shari, I am so sorry for my lies and for cruelty to the dog. If anything happens to Peter and Cody, I'll never forgive myself. But I received Jesus and became a Christian while you were on the phone. So I will pray with you."

"Wonderful!" said Mrs. Miller.

In the meantime, Peter was walking his dog to the nearest truck stop to see if any trucks were bound for Terryville. The walk was long and cold.

On his way he found a school bus taking high school students on a trip. Peter asked the driver, "Are you going through Terryville?"

"Yes we are," answered the man.

"Well my dog and I live there, but we have no way home," said Peter. "The family is worried about me. Would you please give us a ride?"

"I'm sorry," answered the driver. "But no dogs are allowed on this bus."

"Please?" begged Peter. "My dad left him here, and I came and got him. We have no way home."

"No way," said the driver.

When the bus left, Peter said, "Cody, if you don't go home, I don't go home."

The walk to the truck stop was long and cold. When they finally got there, Peter found a truck driver heading for Terryville and asked him for a ride. But the driver said, "I'm sorry, but I have my dog and someone else riding with me. So there's no room."

Back at Peter's house in Terryville, all four of his grandparents had arrived. His parents and grandparents kept kneeling down in prayer for the safe return of Peter and Cody.

While they prayed, Peter and Cody stayed at the truck stop for hours. But no one was going to Terryville. Finally, Peter called the freight yard to see if he could ride the freight train home. But the next train was not going there till after Christmas. None of their trucks were going there either.

It was getting dark. Peter wondered if he and Cody would make it home. If not, where would they sleep? He did not have much cereal, dog food or water left.

To make matters worse, Peter and his dog were tired from hours of walking and waiting. So Peter got on his knees and prayed with tears in his eyes, "Lord Jesus: Please help me and Cody to get home tonight. Amen."

Just then a young girl came along and said, "What's wrong?"

Peter was crying and said, "My dog Cody and I have no way to get home to Terryville. My father left Cody here hoping someone would find him and keep him. So I came here on a truck and got him. But I have no way home because no dogs are allowed on the bus. I also don't have very much money."

"Oh dear," said the girl. "Well, let's be friends. My name is Brenda Wiseman." Shaking hands with her, Peter said, "My name is Peter Miller. This is my dog Cody."

"Hello Peter. Hello Cody. My what a good dog!" said Brenda. "I'll bet my grandfather can help you. He's a pilot. He and his friends have a charter plane service. If you'll get in the car, I'll drive you to the airport."

"Thanks," replied Peter graciously as he and Cody got into her car.

Brenda drove Peter and Cody to the Biller City Airport. She said, "We're having a family reunion at the airport. Grandpa is taking us to Fort Bennett for Christmas tonight."

When they arrived at the airport, Brenda escorted Peter and Cody to her grandfather's office. She said, "Grandpa, this is my friend Peter Miller and his dog Cody. I just met them at the truck stop."

"Well hello Peter. Hello Cody," said the grandfather happily. "I'm Bob Wiseman. What a nice dog! What brings you here?"

Brenda answered, "Peter and Cody need a way home to Terryville."

Peter continued, "My father dumped Cody off here yesterday in hopes that someone else would find him and keep him. So I sneaked out and came here on a truck to get him. But we don't have a way home. I came here with very little food and money. I just had to get my dog back."

"Well I understand," said Grandpa Wiseman. "There's no telling what would have happened to Cody if you hadn't come for him. We are having a Christmas family reunion. We will all fly out tonight to Fort Bennett. If you and Cody will fly with us, we will let you off in Terryville."

"Gee thanks Mr. Wiseman!" said Peter.

"Now give me your telephone number so I can call your parents," said Grandpa Wiseman.

But Peter replied, "If we do that, my daddy will make me leave Cody here. I don't want to do that."

"Peter," said Grandpa Wiseman. "Your daddy broke the law leaving the dog here. Besides that, your family must be worried sick about you. Calling them is the right thing to do."

"Well okay," said Peter. "I'll call them myself." He timidly dialed his parents. When his father answered the phone and heard Peter's voice, he was overjoyed. "Peter!" said Mr. Miller. "Are you and Cody all right?"

"Yes Daddy. We're fine," answered Peter. "We're at the Biller City Airport. I made some friends who will fly us home. Mr. Wiseman has a charter plane service."

Mr. Miller went on saying, "Thank goodness! Your mother and I have been praying with your grandparents for you and Cody to make it home. I'm sorry I lied to you, and I'm so sorry I dumped Cody off in Biller City. I was wrong. You may keep the dog. I am now a Christian."

"Great!" exclaimed Peter. "I forgive you, and I love you. Mr. Wiseman wants to talk to you."

"Mr. Miller," said Grandpa Wiseman. "I'm Bob Wiseman. My family and I are leaving tonight. We will fly Peter and Cody home. Please meet us at the Terryville Airport at 9:30."

"Many thanks to you," said Mr. Miller. "We'll be there."

Pulling some money from his wallet, Grandpa Wiseman said, "Brenda, take Peter to dinner at the restaurant across the street, and let him have whatever he wants. Cody can stay here with us. The plane will leave at 8:15."

Brenda took Peter out to dinner. They had a wonderful time together.

After dinner, Brenda, Peter, and Cody boarded the plane and sat together. The plane had many members of the Wiseman family reunion.

Grandpa Wiseman flew the plane from Biller City to Terryville. The trip home was fun.

At 9:30, the plane landed in Terryville. Peter, Cody, Brenda, and Grandpa Wiseman were greeted by Gary and Shari Miller along with the grandparents. "Thanks for bringing Peter and Cody home!" said Mr. Miller. "Have a Merry Christmas!"

"We are so grateful to you and Brenda," said Mrs. Miller to Grandpa Wiseman.

"Merry Christmas to you all!" replied Brenda and her grandfather. Then they boarded the plane and left Terryville.

"Peter," said Mr. Miller. "I don't blame you for leaving to get Cody. It was wrong of me to go off and leave him. It will never happen again. You may keep your dog. You took good care of him and found a way home for him."

Mr. Miller's father said, "Peter, the family went and got you some extra presents as a reward for bringing Cody home."

"Gee thanks," answered Peter.

Mrs. Miller added, "Peter, be sure to call Al Parker when you get home. He called and asked if you and Cody made it home."

That night, Peter slept with Cody at his side. He prayed, "Lord Jesus: Thanks for keeping Cody safe and for helping me to find him and bring him home. I thank you also that Daddy is now a Christian. Amen."

The next morning, Christmas day was filled with joy for Peter's family. They had a delightful breakfast. Then they opened their presents. Mrs. Miller's parents gave Peter $100.00 along with some of his favorite story books. Mr. Miller's parents gave Peter some of his favorite DVD's and music CD's. Also, Peter's mother and daddy gave him a Bible along with books of his favorite Bible stories. Cody got a present from them, too. They gave him a new doggy bed.

Peter now had a happy Christian family. His father never lied to the family again. He was also never again mean to pets. The Miller family was very nice to Cody. Peter kept him for the rest of his life.

Stephen and Susie Harley

A Special Christmas Greeting

Greetings in the name of our Lord Jesus.

My name is Stephen Harley. Merry Christmas to you all!

Now you too can receive Jesus and become a Christian like Peter Miller's father.

On Christmas day, Jesus Christ, God's only Son, was born to save us. This is because we all sin. That means we disobey God. The punishment for sin is death. But when Jesus Christ died on the cross and rose from the dead, He took the punishment for us. So when we turn from sin and invite Jesus into our lives, Jesus enters our lives, cleanses us from sin, and gives us eternal life. When we let Jesus direct every part of our lives, we receive His full blessing.

Please pray this prayer: "Lord Jesus, I am sorry for all my sins. I turn away from all sin. I acknowledge You as God's only Son. Please come into my heart and cleanse me from all sin. Thank You for eternal life. Please direct everything I do for the rest of my life. Thank You Jesus. Amen."

Congratulations! You are now a child of God!

Also, please remember that pets are God's creation. They need the love and care that Christians have to offer. Please consider adopting a pet if you do not have one. Let God work His kindness to them through you. You will be glad you did.

Ten-year old Peter Miller learns that his dog Cody is stranded in Biller City 250 miles from his home in Terryville. When Peter leaves town and gets his dog, he realizes that he and Cody do not have a way home. He has very little food and money, and the ground is covered with snow. But young Peter is determined that he will not go home without his dog. Surrounded by the prayers of his family, it is a race against time for Peter to find a way home before nightfall. Will he and Cody make it home for Christmas? Read this story of determination, love, repentance and forgiveness.

In 1980, Stephen Harley gave every part of his life to Jesus Christ. He is a graduate of Sul Ross State University of Alpine, Texas. He graduated from Christ For the Nations Institute of Dallas, Texas in 1988. He has also experienced God's love for pets.

Printed in the United States
by Baker & Taylor Publisher Services